Pra.

An Inventory of Abandoned Things

"In *An Inventory of Abandoned Things*, everything is alive. The narrator battles against invaders encroaching on her Florida house—cockroaches, squirrels—at the same time that she grows a daughter inside herself. Kelly Ann Jacobson's careful attention to detail and her ability to capture the tension in every human interaction combine to make a chapbook that is at once bittersweet and captivating."

—SJ Sindu, author of *Blue-Skinned Gods* and *Marriage of a Thousand Lies*

"Kelly Ann Jacobson's *An Inventory of Abandoned Things* catalogues our profligacy and parsimony in our reckonings with the world. Through a series of linked flash fictions, the narrator walks a precarious but necessary tightrope—balancing her need to protect her life, her home, and those whom she loves with the liberating necessity of relinquishing her fears for a larger and more expansive, albeit riskier, life. At the heart of this collection is the narrator's relationship with her daughter, from pregnancy to early toddling, and consequently, her daughter's own relationship to a world that is simultaneously cruel and wondrous, invasive and thrilling. Jacobson asks us to consider how we mitigate risk and shelter those we love from predictable dangers, but more importantly, also how we must embrace the thrill of unwieldy possibility."

—Kerry Neville, author of *Remember to Forget Me* and *Necessary Lies*

An Inventory of Abandoned Things

An Inventory of Abandoned Things

Kelly Ann Jacobson

An Inventory of Abandoned Things © 2021, Kelly Ann Jacobson. All rights reserved. No part of this book may be used or reproduced without consent from the author or publisher except in the case of brief quotations appropriated for use in articles and reviews.

Published by Split/Lip Press
6710 S. 87th St.
Ralston, NE 68127
www.splitlippress.com

ISBN: 978-1-952897-13-9

Cover Design by David Wojciechowski

Editing by Pedro Ramírez

For J, who proved my fears unfounded

Contents

Candles

The third store we visit has been raided. The shelves are like rows of gapped teeth—missing flashlights, missing batteries, missing fans, missing gallon jugs of water. Our list is a prayer in your clasped hands. "What about candles?" you ask, and the nervous girl hanging lighters on the endcap takes us through the aisles to décor. "Not much left," she says as she eyes the few colorful glass cylinders on the shelf. Is she reconsidering her own supply? Will she return here to scavenge the remains? I notice, then, that she has a bump of her own, but I know better than to ask. She retreats back to the lighters, and I watch, out of the corner of my eye, as she bends and hangs and slides.

"Pumpkin spice?" you say as you wave one of the candles under my nose. The smell is cinnamon, clove, and maple—but not pumpkin.

I turn back to you and shake my head. "Please don't ruin pumpkin spice for me."

"I forgot you're an addict." You clink the cylinder holder down and retrieve the pink one. "How about this?" Watermelon, oversweet, like the fruit has turned.

"Worse," I say. My sense of smell has always been stronger than yours, but the extra estrogen in my body has turned me bloodhound. I point to the white ones, Clean Laundry. "Just buy two of those and let's get out of here."

"Fine." Your voice is angry trying to be calm. You are probably thinking, *Why did you bring me here?*

I am thinking it too.

Of course, we never use those candles. Or the one jug of water we find in the cracker aisle at Walmart. Or the sanitary wipes. Or the black beans, baked beans, sliced carrots, peaches in 100% juice, saltines, minestrone soup, all still towered in the back of the cabinet like soldiers ready to deploy at a flicker of the lights. We never use any of them, because we are not there to watch the trees fall against our chain-link fence. *Maybe we should go?*, we vaguely ask our neighbor, a true Tallahassee man, and he says, with his calm voice and waiting-to-catch-a-fish gaze, *I think that would be best.* This is a man who slept through the last hurricane. This is a man who knows how to batten down the hatches with storm shutters and sandbags. He is our litmus test—If the locals are all staying, we tell ourselves, then who cares what the privileged students do?— but that morning, after he tells us what is *best*, we pack our bags and leave within the hour.

We are lucky we find an article about filling up our tank so we can use the car to charge our phones.

We are lucky we don't have a good car, the kind that only takes premium-unleaded, and that we make it all the way to Troy, Alabama without needing to stop at the gas stations, most of which are emptied like breast at the mouths of famished babes and left with plastic bags on the handles like the white flags of surrender. We are lucky, lucky, lucky to be those privileged students; or, rather, for me to be that student, and for you to be that privileged—and don't I feel it, as you swipe your credit card at the desk and I put my hands on my belly and think, *We're safe now.*

Beating Stick

The cockroaches are undead things. Their black bullet bodies come through the space between light switch plate and wall, the hole where a phone line once ran, the crack in the garage room brick. When we open the dishwasher, there they are, babies storming the racks of sticky dishes. Are they coming through the drains? Are they living in the insulation around the machine like lice on a head? You are of one opinion, and I the other, and we are almost louder than the fall of a body from the air vent into your minestrone soup.

Though stupid, the cockroaches manage to escape our descending shoes and newspapers with their frantic scurrying, and we hear them later in the attic beating their translucent wings in the heat. At night, you leave through the back door and take up a wooden pole we found in the shed—a bludgeon that you use to slaughter the roaches perched on the brick. When you reenter, your brow is sweaty and your eyes are wild as the reaper. You have taken life. You will again. The power and the hopelessness of your efforts make you clench your nails into your fists.

"If only we could—"

"Soon." My hands find the baby I will molt like a skin. No pesticides. No chemicals. I wash my hair with a brew of organic shea butter, peppermint oil, and Jamaican black castor oil. Even the radio in my car plays soft classical.

"Not soon enough," you mutter on your way to shower off the remains of your kills.

I would join you, but my brown shampoo sends you into taunts of *dirty hippie*, and I am too tired to survive your scorn. Instead, I return to the laundry hamper to fold your still-warm clothes, and soon spot the brown seed of an egg capsule at the bottom. Between my fingers, the casing of forty eggs feels smooth, like a shell on the beach.

Forty eggs.

Forty lives.

I could save them.

Just a flick of the finger, and this capsule would sail into the cushion of grass behind our porch until the pressure of the hatchlings sends the gray-brown nymphs into the world. The pressure, like a head into a pelvis.

The pressure of her.

These bugs could grow up to carry typhoid fever, I tell myself, or cholera, or the plague. The odds are small, infinitesimally small, but there is not much I can do to protect her from the world. All I can do is this. I fold the capsule into the pages of your Athleta catalog and apply pressure. The capsule collapses into ooze, and quickly I discard the magazine into the trash bag in the kitchen, where some member of the hatchlings' own species might stumble upon the splatter and wonder.

Mama would do anything for you, I tell our baby that night as I listen to the wings beating against the walls. *I would kill for you, and so would Ommi.*

And we would.

And we do.

And back then our motives seem pure, and we beat and beat and beat our stick at the wall, but the pressure of our anger will soon push us out of our capsules, and we will be born again, as hungry and desperate as the undead.

Backpack

The park is empty early on Saturday morning, but the ghosts of the children who played here before still show in the red sand shovel beneath the slide, the *PAW Patrol* water bottle on the bench, and the fuzzy red hat with dangling Pippi Longstocking braids laid over the windowsill of the small wooden house where children hit sticks against the walls and draw silly pictures and bounce balls and in general just release all of their repressed domestic urges from home. I spray sunscreen and lemon eucalyptus oil on Skye, who you have nicknamed Sara, and then on us, two sentries waiting to catch a two year old who might, at any moment, step off the metal structure into the abyss of empty air between her and the fireman's pole. The bottles return to my backpack until the next park trip; in the meantime, they will mingle with half-eaten biscuits, loose raisins, and the other general detritus that makes me smell like compost whenever I wear it.

"She doesn't know her own limits," you say as Skye holds onto the sidebars and looks down the pole.

"That's what I love about her. Anyway, she's much better than she used to be." When you turn around, I nod no very slowly to Skye, and she backs away from the gap.

"I saw that." You try to tickle me in the stomach, but I evade you.

"How do you think Skye will feel about having a security analyst for an Ommi?" I tease.

"Secure."

We move to the sand pit, otherwise known as a volleyball court, and I remove my shoes. The sand is moist, and I try not to think of all of the other feet that have traipsed across this terrain.

"I can't do it again." You stand in the tufts of grass outside the wooden frame and look down at us while Skye begins to shovel sand over my feet. "That sand makes my skin crawl."

"Trust me, I get it," I say, and my feet are two groundhogs making tunnels forward and backward. "But the good news is we haven't ever found any needles. Or condoms."

You look at Skye, but she is too busy dragging a stick through the sand to worry about a single, unimportant word. Strange to think she only knows this place—this capital amidst the panhandle swamp—and that D.C. will stay a skyline poster on her wall.

"Whoops." I shrug my shoulders and unearth my feet.

We go back to the playground, and this time Skye puts her hands in the first holds of a rock wall and declares, "Up!"

"No." You cross your arms. "Absolutely not."

Skye gets her feet onto the lowest holds, and then the next, and begins to spider up the wall in complete defiance of your *No.* When she reaches my waist I put my hands on her butt, ready to hoist her or catch her or fall with her, and then up I go too, one hand holding my body to the wall and the other helping our daughter ascend. I marvel at her strength and determination; she is the best parts of us, both analytical and bold. At one point she looks down, but I don't, because the truth is that I am afraid of heights and if I look down my arms will jelly and then release. "Hi, Ommi!" she says, and you exhale deeply from behind my left shoulder. I wonder what your face looks like. I wonder if you think I will drop her.

"Almost there!" I say, and Skye hooks her grasping fingers into the holes of the upper level. She pulls and pulls, and her body slides out of my grasp like it once left my womb. I am brave behind her, and then we stand, triumphant and out of reach.

The Drey

For over a year, the squirrels are balls rolling across the rafters of the attic, their patter feet chasing in a tireless game of tag. I do not know why we let them stay. Maybe they become a part of the landscape, like the ivy twining onto the brick or the spiders in the empty flowerpots in the shed; maybe we have bigger problems. Until I walk out of the front door and look up to see the rat head of a mama squirrel eyeing me from a new hole in the soffit, this particular house issue seems benign, even comforting, on the nights when you travel away from me.

But I have seen the high black eyes. Something must be done.

The man who comes at my call is in sales. He wears a suit, and his bulky body cannot fit through the access door in Skye's closet. "We can fix this," he says, though he has only a general notion of what *this* is. "Change out the soffits, install a one-way-door, clean up the mess, and," he claps his hands together, "problem solved."

We are never given what we are promised.

The man who comes at his call is the exterminator, and he looks like his prey: small and sideways glancing and always showing up when he hopes we will not be home. In goes the one-way door; up goes not a replacement of soffits, but a stapling of chicken wire across the problem areas and a quick application of spray paint. One by one the squirrels fall through the door and into the palm tree growing too close to the house, which at some point we must find the time to move, and scamper into the nearest live oak. "I'll be back in a week," he says, "to check on things."

We only make it two days.

The squirrels have become diggers scraping away at the soffits. They have made two new holes. They are trying to go home. They are making the master bedroom into a construction site, and I can't write. I tell him these things as I stare, from the ground, at the mama squirrel affixed to the soffit with arms and legs splayed wide and teeth gnawing. So desperate. So fearless. I want to throw a stone, to say *This is my house*, but I am not that brave.

Again, the soffits are covered.

Again, we hear *back in a week*.

A few days later, as I type in the oddly quiet master bedroom, something booms its way from the kitchen down the hall. I freeze. Boom. Boom. Long pause. Boom. Someone is trying to break into the house. My hands shake. I grab my cell phone and leave 9-1-1 entered, but I do not hit dial, just carry the phone and a heavy flashlight I keep by my bed as a weapon down the hallway.

No one is at the door.

No one is in the yard.

Boom.

Boom, boom, boom.

The sound is coming from the vent above the stove.

Wait.

A squirrel is trapped *inside* the vent above the stove.

Now 9-1-1 becomes the exterminator. "They are coming in," I say, my voice wild, "One of them is in the stove vent. Do you hear that? The booming? What if they get inside?"

"They won't," he promises, and tells me he can come tomorrow, as if this is not an emergency and I am not in danger and the squirrel is not going to break free or die of starvation inside of the vent in the meantime. After he hangs up, I am tempted to unscrew the vent—the poor creature—but then I think about the time my mom walked through a park wearing brown shorts as a child, and the squirrels climbed up her legs and left claw marks like knives plunged into soft butter.

I end up securing the vent with duct-sealing tape instead.

By the time tomorrow comes, the squirrel has escaped. The exterminator puts wire mesh over the vent cap, and removes the one-way door, and sincerely apologizes but at our price point he cannot actually access the squirrel nest and the shit and the nuts growing old in the attic. The salesman is new, and he has been talked to, and they are both very sorry.

"What about the squirrels?" I ask. "Won't they keep trying to get in?"

"Probably." He swings his clipboard under his arm. "Don't forget that this is their home."

I feel this judgment whenever I see the squirrel family in the live oak or when they descend every morning and early evening to forage. At least, I think they are the same family, though I soon realize the whole neighborhood is full of these rodents. But what could we have done differently? Left to their own devices, they might have chewed through the wires, or left enough excrement to rot the wood, or died up there like Miss Emily and been found a year later from the smell.

"What could we have done differently?" I ask when I pick you up at the airport.

"Nothing. You're overthinking this, Elora. Let it go."

You do not understand. You are fresh from D.C., and you would readily put up the For Sale sign and move back today if only I would hurry up and graduate. You even smell like the other house, the vanilla air freshener and the backyard fern garden and the sheets under which you enjoyed your uninterrupted sleep. No squirrels. No Skye. No roaches. No alerts from the Arlo system we set up after those men cased our house.

You do not understand, because you have not had to claw at the soffit, day after day, until the metal hairs give way and the light narrows into a hole behind you and there, in its leafy glory, is your nest.

The Mask

After my late-night fiction workshop, I come home tired and sore-legged from sitting for so long in the same chair to find the house transformed into a stifled box of waterborne urethane air from day three of our floor-refinishing project. The windows have been left closed—this is Florida, after all—but I open them now and let the oppressive humidity layer over the VOCs.

According to the contractor, whom I text in my panic, over the past three days the layers of finishing have soaked into the wood and now have nowhere to emit their fumes but up. He assures me that the VOC level of this product is low—that is why we picked a waterborne urethane finish in the first place—and that the smell should dissipate soon. *Thanks*, I write, and go to the screened-in porch to wait.

Immediately bored, I call you and tell you about the smell, and then the cockroach confidently scurrying toward my glass full of apple juice; I try not to sound resentful when I ask why we timed this renovation during one of your trips. You tell me about D.C., and send me a picture of the Washington Monument at night.

I delete it.

When I go back inside, the smell is the same as before, only worse, because now I have a headache.

You could sleep in the mask, you suggest, so I go to the closet in the garage room and find the gray respirator. In the selfie I send you, I look like Leia impersonating a bounty hunter in *Return of the Jedi*, and you text back *Elora the Hut*, which is a more accurate description. I laugh and forget that the VOCs in the air can cause birth defects, low birth weight, and premature births. Then I remember.

Our bed is in the living room, surrounded by windows without curtains, so I prop myself up with pillows and stare at the panes of dusty glass and wait for sleep—or for an intruder to set off the siren of our home security system. A few weeks ago, our house was cased by young men with a white van, and our neighbors, in low voices, confess that the house had been broken into before. *There were guns in a safe,* they say, *and they took all of them.* Now there is nothing in the house to steal, and yet I watch the windows and worry every time the lights from a passing car look like the heads of flashlights pressed to the panes. At some point, I fall asleep.

In the middle of the night, I startle awake to the feeling of a hand over my mouth, so I claw at my face and find the soft filters of the mask, the plastic face piece, and the rubber strap. I can't breathe, and my heart is pounding as fast as the baby's. When I get up, I trigger the alarm, which wails its siren song until I turn off the Arlo on my phone app. My heart beeps out an S.O.S. in Morse code. When I check the time, I can't believe it is only 2:00 AM, and there are still seven more hours until I have to teach.

Sleep will not happen, so I go back out to the porch and turn on the lights to ward off all but the bravest cockroaches. I open up the text chain under *Jane* but decide not to wake you up—you have to work in the morning, and besides, I am the one who got us into this mess in the first place—and instead I wonder what a thief would think if he found me here, legs up on the wrought iron patio table, belly out to my knees, head lying back on the chair, in a white men's undershirt and basketball shorts. I wonder if I should write a short story about all of this, but decide that it would be a murder, and that is the last thing I need to imagine right now.

The morning sun brings with it a dim view of our neighbor's butterfly garden, and because I have nothing else to do, I watch. The insects dart, land, dart, turning the land into a series of stop-motion frames, while squirrels intrude and then disappear up the palm tree trunks. The gopher tortoise she keeps as a pet leaves his burrow and paddles his way to the lettuce left in a plastic lid. Later he might bob his head to entice the gardening hose, or inspect the corner where the house meets the stone wall holding him inside.

Soon the sun pulls off the lens cap of darkness and morning arrives. I breathe the clean air and marvel at the fact that this time three months ago I was at home—my other home—sitting in the traffic right before Rosslyn wondering if there would be a spot in my usual lot.

I have sanded off the top layer of my life, I tell myself as I take another deep breath and let the air fill my polluted lungs, *but I will paint over it, coat by coat. I will make it beautiful.*

The tortoise taunts me with his dance, and I shake my head too. *Fine. You win, gopher tortoise.*

Life is already beautiful, and I am the one who needs to be sanded down to dust.

Blanket

The beer pressed against my cheek sweats tears down the side of my face and onto our picnic blanket, where the droplets mingle with the crumbs of a quiche crust and evaporate. We are in our usual spot under the live oak, from which we have the best view of the children dancing like wild beasts in front of the raised stage, but even the shade cannot shield us from the sun still battling for its time in the wide blue sky. You are eating fries from the food trucks, and I am sneaking bites of a black bean burrito from my purse whenever the hired guard turns away.

"Look!" You point to the right side of the stage, where Skye has suckerfished her hands to the stage and is now bobbing like the pedal of a drum. "She's incredible!"

You haven't seen her dance, or push her own stroller across the rolling lawn, or work the crowd so that each patron gives her a piece of pizza, an apple, a fruit snack. You haven't been home in time, but today you arrive in your suit carrying a six pack of beer and find an unstained place on the blanket to perch. At least you take off your shoes, your blazer, the pins holding your bun in place. A dancer at the front might survey the crowd and skip over you, though the doubtful expression with which you watch the middle-aged hippies swing their skirts might trigger suspicion.

"I told you that girl has natural rhythm," I say.

Worried that Skye might go for the power cords snaked in wait around the stage, I get up with effort and cross through the chaos of balls and hula hoops to our daughter, who does not notice me.

The woman on stage a few feet from us does, though, and she winks at me before bending to bestow her instrument on Skye. The motion required for the jingles is too advanced for a one year old, but our daughter bangs the skin stretched over the frame happily as the band members laugh at their newest addition.

Eventually, Skye abandons the drum and totters away toward Lake Ella. My friend, the one who invited us so long ago that Food Truck Thursday has become a regular part of our week, comes to where I stand and suggests that I let her go. "She'll turn around before too long," she promises. "But if you chase her, she'll feel safe and just keep on walking."

Why not try it, I think, and I do not chase her. She keeps on walking anyway. Through the people watching from the outskirts. Over the cement divider. She doesn't even look back, just pumps her arms and wide legs like a determined mall walker.

"I'm surprised," says my friend.

"She doesn't care if I'm chasing her or not," I explain as I prepare to run. And I love that about her.

But I am also afraid.

Terrarium

I am on the phone with you when I close the closet door and feel the abrupt stick of the hinge push back against my hand. "What the . . . ?" I say, having closed and opened that door three times that day, and then I notice the anole trapped by its left leg like a cow hung after slaughter. Its toe pads paddle against the door. "Oh my god," I say, and swing the door back, loosening the poor creature enough to send it plummeting to the hardwood floor. "Oh my god, oh my god, oh my god."

Luckily, you are a keeper of strange pets, and our gecko's travel terrarium is still in the garage closet. I cup the anole into the terrarium and then, on your instructions, fill the tank with a fake fern, newspaper ads, and a dish of water. I try not to make direct eye contact with the leg, which is cut to the bone like a Thanksgiving turkey, but my gaze keeps drifting back.

I did this.

The creature will not survive.

"Get some sleep," you tell me. "It's midnight, and there's nothing else you can do."

I change into a men's undershirt and boxers, the cheapest sleep garments to fit over my expanding belly, and crawl into bed. Instead of sleeping, however, I scroll through internet chats about wounded anoles and how if I find one I should immediately take it to a veterinarian. *Vet, vet, vet,* I think as I type, *animal hospital, 24-hour, emergency.* Northwood Animal Hospital, just five minutes away via Monroe Street, pops up. I dial the number, and they tell me that yes, they can take an anole, and they even serve as a drop-off point for St Francis Wildlife Rescue.

I am out of bed and in the car before I hang up.

At Northwood, a friendly nurse comes at the buzz and asks me to fill out an intake form. She takes my anole crisis very seriously, nods and smiles and tells me that I absolutely did the right thing by bringing it, and yet I am suddenly self-conscious about wasting her time. "I hope it's okay," I tell her as she moves the anole to a cardboard box she dug up from somewhere in the back, and she assures me that it will be. I wonder what I look like to her, eight months pregnant and wearing a men's undershirt, and decide that she has probably seen worse.

I am still thinking about the anole when I get to class the next morning. As soon as everyone sits, I launch into my story, sure to include the terrible angle of the leg and the relief I felt as I handed the anole over to the competent nurse.

"That's so cute," one of my students says, and I ask why. "Well," she says, suddenly self-conscious now that she speaks for the class, "it's just that anoles are like mice here. We flush them down the toilet when we find them. The thought of you bringing one to an animal hospital . . . " She cracks up, and the class joins her, a bunch of native Floridians who would no sooner take a wounded anole to a hospital than I would a cockroach with a missing wing.

This act of kindness has marked me as other. I move on to the lesson, aware that my students now think of me as "cute," and yet, when I think back on this night later, I will feel more a part of the landscape than ever before—not antagonistic, not apathetic, but active, a working piece of this strange city where anoles stop-motion animate across the bright green palmettos and humans are wounds cut to the bone over which nature must heal.

Apple Pie

On move-in day, our neighbors come to the door with a pie. We eye them, two strangers bearing friendly smiles and their dessert, through the peephole. "Do you know them?" you whisper, and I, with my big belly pressed against the cold metal door, say no. I have only been here once, for inspection day, though perhaps these neighbors spied on me from their window the way we are watching them now. The man is tall and narrow, and he wears a large cross around his neck. The woman's face belongs on packaging, the proclamation of *mother* written everywhere from her curly hair to her birth stone jewelry. Or maybe it's just that she's holding a pie.

"Welcome!" they say as the door swings open, and here comes the gift, with an apology that the pie is not homemade. There was no time, I must see, because their daughter and her family temporarily live with them and the grass had to be cut, and oh, I'm pregnant, how wonderful, they need new blood around here. The pie is heavy, at least three pounds, and the plastic container creases at the place where my fingertips hold its bulk. *Half of a small baby*, I think, balancing the other end of the container on my hip.

They do not mention joining them for service, though the man is a pastor, and for this we are grateful. There will be plenty of times, later, when these offers will catch us by surprise. For now, we commune here in our empty hallway, the camping chairs and air mattress behind us, signs that though we have moved in we have not *moved*. Our things still take up space in the D.C. apartment, where two transient State Department employees currently reside, and then a librarian, and then a lobbyist, and then, if all goes according to plan, us again.

"Ya'll come by anytime!" they say, and when we close the door we stare at our new pie in wonder. Back in D.C. we know only one neighbor, and only because she called the police about a noise disturbance at 9:00 PM. Mary Jane Briar, earliest sleeper in the nation's capital.

"Well, that was weird," you say, your non-accent noticeable only by comparison, and I agree as I slide my finger under the plastic lid and break the label. All for me. I retrieve a plastic fork from last night's takeout bag and dive into the wet layers of crust, apple, crust, then taste cinnamon and brown sugar mixed with sweet apple chunks. A homemade pie would have a harder shell, having not sat on a factory shelf and then a store table soaking in its juices, but I still manage to eat a quarter of it before storing it safely in the refrigerator. No roaches there—at least not yet.

"We really are in the south," I say, our Florida armpit turning out to be more Georgia than Sunshine State.

"Amen," you say with an eye roll.

Two years later, an identical pie sits on our counter, greened from mold and browned in the places where liquid has compromised the crust. For my new neighbors, I'd thought when I'd seen the display by the grocery store door, and I really had intended to walk across the street and say welcome. But you see, there was no time, and I had thirty-eight final papers to grade and Mother's Day brunch at Skye's daycare where I had to be two mothers instead of one and Zumba class, and oh, I guess you can take the girl out of D.C. but you can't take the D.C. out of the girl, am I right?

Then again, two years ago I would not have bought the pie.

And when I see the new neighbors, I will wave and say hello, and if they are from up north, they will squint suspiciously and mumble "Hey" and quicken their pace.

And after a big storm, I will help them move the oak branch off their driveway.

And when their dog gets loose, I will carry him back, tongue licking at my neck like an overzealous lover.

I will be my version of a good neighbor, and I will think, afterward, that I like this person who babysits a child for a sick mother and finally invites her friend in for tea and buys pies, even uneaten ones, because she wants to make someone feel at home.

Can I get an amen?

Cow Baby

The riverboat glides through the water of the Wakulla like the efficient sandpiper skimming the surface of the ocean, and I, accompanied by nineteen other tourists and a local guide, am gently propelled downstream through the right lane of the loop. Spotting alligators becomes our game—*Look at that one!*, *Oh my god!*, *To your right!*—as we settle for the grin of a sunning crocodilian in the absence of any marine mammals. "Old Joe," our guide begins as we snap cell phone pictures of young Joes, "was an 11-foot gator famous for his docile temperament until a poacher shot him in 1966. At that point, locals thought he was 200 years old." I wonder at this naming, this singling out of one among so many, and am even more surprised when the guide tells us that a stuffed Old Joe still resides in a glass display in the lodge. *Typical Florida*, I think as I snap, snap, snap.

When we reach the end of the loop and turn, I spot motion to my left. A gray boulder rises to the surface and paddles gently. "A manatee!" a boy behind me proclaims, and we are all one organism craning our neck to see the sea cow snout poking up from the water. More appear, surprisingly graceful as they emerge and dive. *I know how you feel*, I think as I pat my own straining bump, only eased in the water to a slight tug when I do laps at the school gym.

The manatees sink, but their presence lingers in the blurred shadows of the water. The guide tries to entice us with more alligators, osprey, a white ibis, but we sit back in our seats and suffer the aftershocks of awe. To be so close to something so incredible as a manatee, and then to go on with our lives, the daily grind of grading and emails and meetings, seems impossible. Or maybe I'm projecting. A tourist in high socks and a fanny pack takes the ibis bait and raises her camera.

After the tour ends, I climb the diving tower and look down at the dark shadow of the vent from which aquifer water seeps. The thought of the cool depth makes me shiver. A swimming area has been roped off, but who would venture there after what we have seen?

Before leaving the lodge, I buy future Skye a stuffed animal manatee, which she will later name Cow Baby. Cow Baby will sit in her car seat during daycare hours and will be there, waiting, when she returns to the car covered in dirt and dried paint. Cow Baby will sleep beached against the crib bars. Cow Baby will have its own carrier, fashioned from a pillowcase and two strings, with which Skye will cart the creature around the neighborhood until an accident sends Cow Baby plummeting into a puddle.

Every time I pat Skye to sleep, I will lay my other hand on Cow Baby's short fur, nothing like the thick skin of a real manatee, and remember that day at Wakulla. My awe will not wane after two years, mingled, as it will become, with the curled boulder of a baby drifting down into the cavernous vent of sleep.

Insect Killer

I.

"The ant's a centaur in his dragon world." —Ezra Pound, "Canto LXXXI"

II.

As I pause, one leg over the driver's seat and the other grounded on the driveway pavement, I happen to look down to the mat, the moving mat, the mat alive with ants on their pilgrimage, and then to the cup holder where half of a melted meal replacement bar feeds its devotees with chocolate life. "Holy shit," I scream as I do the pregnant woman equivalent of a backward jump, really more of an airy step, into the door. My cell phone shakes in my hand as I call you until you pick up. "I'm on a call," you say, and I say, "There are ants in my car, like the bad kind, all over the car, what do I do?"

I am supposed to be on the way to my doctor's appointment, I am supposed to be standing on a scale and making sure that all of these between-meal bars and chalky drinks have worked, and instead I am under attack.

"You mean fire ants?"

"Sure, yes, the red ones." I peer in again. "The ones that bite." Then I look down and realize a few of their scouts are on the door, so I smoosh them under my finger. "This is a serious emergency."

You tell me to just use the insecticide, and I remind you that I am growing a baby human and cannot just use the insecticide, that using the insecticide could cause some horrible birth defect that I can't specify because I don't actually know but that is definitely serious and life-threatening, and that you have to come home right now and deal with this.

"I'm in D.C."

Right. Another work trip. I hang up without saying good-bye—I can get away with these things now—and crouch down so far that my belly touches my thighs. "Die, you assholes," I say as I smoosh, smoosh, smoosh until armor plates my fingertips. Then I get a piece of paper with some old gum wrapped inside and launch a full-fledged war. Ten. Fifteen. Ants flee from my descending hand. I know that this method of attack is futile, that twenty ants out of five hundred won't make a difference, but I have lost control. The paper is rusty red.

Suddenly, the car is empty.

I check under the mat, and a few stragglers meet their end at my vengeful hand. I check the cup holder. The ants have disappeared, leaving no trace except the sticky chocolate bar, which goes into a plastic bag and then the trash bin.

On the drive to the doctor's, I puzzle over this phenomenon. I also realize that I probably parked on a crack in the driveway, under which an ant mound found itself under attack by a weighty tire and surged upward only to find a delicious surprise instead, and that maybe you were right when you told me a million times that fire ants would not invade the house—that such behaviors were not standard practice for creatures that prefer open areas, and no, they would not murder the rabbits, and could I please close my eyes and go to sleep for god's sake, and wasn't I the one who wanted to move here in the first place?—but that I don't care.

I am going to kill them all anyway.

III.

By the time I find ants in the mailbox, I have grown accustomed to the fight-or-flight surge of norepinephrine and epinephrine that comes with most days here. I still drop the junk mail delivered at some point over the past two weeks, but I do not scream. Plus, these ants are black, small, and as far as I can tell, using my barely balanced box as a home for their nursery, and I do not want to scare Skye unnecessarily.

"Looks like you got yourself some sugar ants," says a man walking his basset hound from the street behind me.

"Has this happened to you?"

"To everyone."

I put the mail back and close the lid.

That night, in the sparse glow of the distant streetlights, I calmly aim my wand and pump.

IV.

A line of carpenter ants congas down the live oak trunk, up the corner of the house, and across the soffit to a hole that was once wood. For two months they will dance their continuous dance, and then they will finish whatever dead thing they have found and move on.

Umbrella Holder, Always Empty

Nothing comes as close to The Flood as a rainy day in Florida. I sit on the screened-in porch at the end of our six-seater wrought iron table with my feet up and the back of my head, the occipital bone, resting on the top rail, as I watch the sky cry onto the plastic leaves of the palm trees that divide our yard from the neighbor's. The drops add their masses to the sandy puddles where grass should be, where, when all of this water has evaporated, bald dirt will play house to red ant piles and tree roots and poison ivy tendrils. No point worrying about the yard, you keep saying. In a few years, this shit hole will be someone else's problem.

My eyes close, and I focus on the sound, the mike static, of the rain and the family of squirrels in the trees and the plugged gutter drooling a line of water while the rest slides off the roof in sheets. We keep meaning to clean the gutters—we even borrowed our neighbor's ladder to do it—and yet the leaves clump the hole like hair in a drain and will, again, tomorrow.

On the table are my unopened textbooks. Funny, that I play recorded rain to help me focus, yet now I can't bring myself to read a page. My eyes return to the rain, the leaves, the neighbor's butterfly garden, and there is her son, coming around the house, tapping on the bathroom window. He is in his fifties, a good-looking man, full head of hair and jeans that fit well. He comes by a lot, but usually through the front door.

Now he is at the kitchen window.

Now he is in the back door.

Maybe the neighbor is partially deaf. Maybe the sound of rain is like static in her hearing aid. Maybe she is dead. I wonder these things, wonder if I should get up and help, but I can't do that either. My body feels waterlogged—is waterlogged, if not from the splattered rain getting through the screens then from the humidity, which has turned the air solid like pudding thickening in a pot. I should invite him in. I should offer my umbrella.

Then I remember that my umbrella is lost, and my raincoat is at school, and my boots are in the car behind the passenger seat, and I think instead, I should buy an extra pair. I should buy a few more umbrellas. Not a waste of money, since rain is a certainty here, and besides, I can't keep showing up to class wet. I can use them in the future. After all, there will still be rain in D.C. when I get back . . .

. . . just not *this* rain.

After a few minutes, the back door opens and out comes the neighbor, bewildered by the wet dog of a man shaking off the rain and stomping the mud from his shoes. She is still wearing her pajamas at 3:00 PM, a long blue nightgown and slippers, and her hair is dry under a plastic cap. *I was in the shower*, I imagine her telling her son. That explains it.

There is only an hour left until I have to pick Skye up from daycare, so I open up a book on early book printing and skim a few damp pages, put the book down, pick it up again. The rain is like an audience clapping, and I am the speaker soaking it all up, not yet able to raise my hand or clear my throat and say "You're too kind." *There will be rain*, I think again, but the fact feels like a lie.

Finally, after another ten minutes, the rain stops all at once. My ears buzz in the relative silence. The leaves still drip, but now they are accompanied by car wheels zipping over wet roads, birds chirping in the palm trees, and the family of squirrels eager to sun their wet tails. The son comes out to dry the patio chairs, and then he and his mother sit and mutter over tall glasses of iced tea. The afternoon is saved.

This is why I can't go inside on rainy days, I think, balancing my book on my knees. Nothing comes as close to The Flood—or The Rapture.

Reclaimed Table

The van rattles over the dips of the southernmost end of the Red Hills Region, and every time the doors quake against their hinges, we jump. "I hate this van," you mutter, "I hate these hills, I hate Tallahassee, I hate—"

"There." I point to a road sign bent backward so that the white letters of the street name almost touch the ground, a full limbo, likely knocked over during the winds of Michael. You yank the wheel, and we just miss the iron plants around a neighbor's mailbox. Deep breath. These people would notice a few missing leaves; we are in the nice quadrant of the city, northeast, where the grass is green and full and there are no cars held in place by dusty red bricks. I feel out of place in my old T-shirt and yoga pants, slouch down in my seat.

"Remind me why we didn't buy a house in *this* part of Tallahassee?" you ask.

"$100,000."

"Right."

This settles you, but I am still wondering as we pass brick ranch, gray-sided ranch, brick ranch. Hard to say what is different, exactly; new paint, of course, and new roofs, but also the small things, like mower lines and shrubs trimmed back into shapely balls. They sport university flags, but new ones, with the garnet background not yet dusted into the brown-red of dried blood. If these Floridians have boats, they must keep them in their sheds.

"Next one, right after that live oak."

You turn into 1847, a gray ranch with white shutters. Two sprinklers work at once, even though we will get our daily rain at 3:00 PM on the dot, with a third visible in the backyard as we pull up to the garage. In our neighborhood, most of the garages have been converted into extra rooms, done cheaply with a wall knocked down and the original door filled in with telltale siding. As we climb down from the van, a dog barks from inside the house, its sound menacing until we meet its slobbery face at the screen door. "Down, Buster. Down, boy."

The woman's voice turns into a body, dressed for going out—or maybe this is how people always dress in this neighborhood. Fitted jeans, flouncy white top, hair curls, full face of makeup. Ready to run for Miss Florida. Her husband follows her, and I realize it has been a long time since I've seen a man with a good haircut. When he opens the door, the first thing I spot is an oversized canvas print of their family, four perfect brunettes and Buster, hung on the nearby hallway wall.

"I can help carry the table, but . . . " The man looks behind us for the missing husband hiding in the van.

"Me too," you say, and hold his gaze.

I stay with the wife and make small talk. How old are your children? She says five and seven, the boy a star football player already and little Gracie Jean learning to pirouette and jeté. My daughter is six months, I say, still working on more sitting than second position. You danced? she asks, and I say yes, a long time ago, in what feels like another life. We talk about tap, and then the Seminoles, and then finally here comes the table, as big and sturdy as the craigslist photos made it out to be.

"Get the chairs, Elora?" you huff, and I can tell you are struggling to keep up your end of the reclaimed pine table. I am grateful to have something to do, and for the excuse to see the kitchen, which is all white and spotless, even the floor. Unused pots hang above the island like wind chimes. A threshold blessing states Jeremiah 29:11: "'FOR I KNOW THE PLANS I HAVE FOR YOU,' DECLARES THE LORD, 'PLANS TO PROSPER YOU AND NOT TO HARM YOU, PLANS TO GIVE YOU HOPE AND A FUTURE.'" And a trust fund, I think as I examine its neighbor, another picture of the boy and girl in the same outfits as the hallway portrait.

The woman and I both take two chairs. The wood is soft and the finish buttery, so that if I pressed my nail into the top rail, I would leave a mark. This is a table that has served every square meal for years, and I imagine them, all four perfect owners, with their heads bowed over their plates in prayer, as I walk back down the hallway.

You and the man are inside the van, so they take the chairs from us and stack them on top of the table. "I'll get the last two chairs," I say, so this time I walk through the house alone, feeling even more like a voyeur than before. I imagine living here. I want to live here. I did live here, once, in what feels like a different life.

After you hand over the $200, we drive back across town in silence. I am thoughtful; you are seething. Apparently, the man called you "surprisingly strong." This irks me, but less so than you, and besides, I am busy imagining how different our life would be if we moved northeast.

When we get home, we unload the table and chairs quickly—only twenty minutes left on our rental—and then you speed off, leaving me to arrange our fruit in the metal bowl I bought at Goodwill that morning to decorate this very table. I carefully place the bowl center right, where a red stain from the previous owners gives away that this new table is not so new. I slide the bowl over an inch. Back an inch. Forward. Maybe a runner would be better. Yes, definitely, a wide runner. You are still gone, so I pull the highchair from the kitchen into the living room and press the lip up to the table. Maybe I should buy holiday runners and switch them out, and matching napkins. Do people still use cloth napkins? Tablecloths?

You come back, and we make celebratory mint juleps and bring them to the new table. "Use a coaster," I tell you, but then I remember our coasters are back in the D.C. apartment, so we use folded pieces of paper.

"Good call," you say as you pick up your drink and peel off the paper already wet from condensation. "If we keep the table in good condition, we can leave it for future renters. Call the place 'partially furnished.' We won't need the beds either, right? Or the desks?"

"Right," I say. Then I take a long sip of my drink and then put it down, sans paper, on the soft, buttery finish.

Five Paint Samples Stacked in the Closet, Perpetually Dripping

This is the state of our kitchen in spring 2020:

The white subway tile floor sports dusty footprints and water drops that turn the smooth surface into a frozen pond. I fell once, crying for fear that I had hurt the baby, and will fall again by the end of the semester. There are cracks between the tiles and the cabinets, where you have plugged the way with a yellow foam sealant so that the cockroaches, still living at the time, must use the outlets. The cabinets smell like their floral paper and are mostly empty. *Funny how much storage we have here*, we tell our visitors, *when back home we had to buy a bed with rolling drawers beneath just to put away our towels*. The dishwasher is new, the refrigerator and stove old, the microwave dragged down from my parents' house in our first carload. The lights are replacements, still long panels like in high school hallways but at least functional.

There are five paint circles of varying shades of white on the far wall.

They have been there since November.

The problem is not the similarity of "Cup of Cream" and "Cotton Ball," although this is a secondary problem. Where do cups of cream and cotton balls fall on the spectrum of moon to coast? How do any of these words convey the boring whitish-tan options in front of me? But even before this crisis of vocabulary comes the crisis of intention, and this conundrum brings us to the state of our kitchen in spring 2020.

For *whom* am I making this choice?

I try to imagine the future renters—or buyers, don't rule out buyers—sitting at the island in a year. They are locals, and they own a boat. They say words like "ya'll" and "pretty as a peach." They are uncomfortable in anything but T-shirts and shorts. They bring their own solo cups full of vodka and Coke to parties. They have a dog, a Pit Bull, that is always getting out and terrorizing the neighborhood.

Or maybe they are a newly hired Assistant Professor and her family, not yet ready to buy in the right part of town, but also not willing to share an apartment building with her students. The big yard will be important, the vintage feel of the pink bathroom tiles, the number of good reading spots.

Or maybe they are four undergrads, sorority girls who decorate the place for Christmas and let their visiting friends sleep on a futon in the garage room.

Or maybe they are me.

Acknowledgments

My years in Tallahassee had many challenges, and thus there are many people I would like to thank. Firstly, thank you to my friends, especially Heather and Ösel, for your support during what would have been a very lonely time. Thank you to my neighbors—you know who you are—who became my Tallahassee family. Thank you to the staff at Bright Star Kid Care for taking such wonderful care of my daughter (and me, at times!), and to Kristy, who made it possible for me to attend late night classes and listened to "Baby Shark" more times than I can count. Thank you to my professors at Florida State—especially Ravi, Mark, and Elizabeth—for always supporting my writing experiments. Finally, thank you to judge Brenna Womer, who selected this strange little book out of the many wonderful submissions, and to the team at Split/Lip—especially Kristine, Pedro, David, and Caleb—for all of your hard work.

About the Author

Kelly Ann Jacobson is the author of many published novels for both adults and young adults, and her short fiction has been published in such places as *Northern Virginia Review, Iron Horse Literary Review, Gargoyle*, and *Best Small Fictions 2020*. Kelly is a PhD candidate in fiction at Florida State University and teaches speculative fiction for Southern New Hampshire University's online MFA in creative writing. More information about her can be found at www.kellyannjacobson.com.

Now Available From

Split/Lip Press

For more info about the press and our titles, visit

www.splitlippress.com

Follow us on Twitter and Instagram: @splitlippress

Made in the USA
Monee, IL
24 February 2023

27930202R00030